Adapted by Marc Cerasini

Based on the series created by

Mark McCorkle & Bob Schooley

New York

CHAPTER 1

Scoop Stoppable

Kim Possible was totally tweaked.

When she opened her locker door, she found sheets and sheets of paper rolling off her computer printer. And she had *just* refilled the paper tray!

But she hadn't commanded her computer to print. So who had? she wondered.

A page fluttered in front of her face. She reached out to catch it.

"Don't touch that!" Ron Stoppable, Kim's

best friend, cried. He snatched the paper out of her hand.

"No offense, K.P., but that's very sensitive material," said Ron. He quickly emptied the printer.

"Really?" Kim said doubtfully. She was still mad that he'd used up all of her paper.

Rufus, Ron's pet naked mole rat, climbed out of Ron's pocket and squinted at the pages.

"Hmmmm," squeaked Rufus curiously.

But Ron snatched the pages away and waved them in front of Kim's nose.

"It's a story I'm writing for the school paper," he told her. "Hard-hitting stuff!"

"You're not *on* the paper, Ron," Kim said flatly. "They keep turning you down."

Ron frowned.

"No offense," Kim added. She honestly wasn't trying to make Ron feel bad. She just wanted him to face reality.

"This story is going to turn them around," said Ron. "It's an edgy exposé."

But Kim wasn't so sure.

Later that day, Ron met with the editor of the school newspaper. He presented her with his latest "hard-hitting" news story.

The editor took the pages and read the headline aloud: *"Math: You'll Never Actually Use It in the Real World."*

The editor rolled her eyes. She had a new headline for him: *Not Interested*.

But Ron refused to give up. "I'm already working on a follow-up piece about semi-colons," he said.

The editor stood up and pointed at Ron.

"Ron—" she began.

Suddenly, the telephone rang.

"News desk!" the editor barked into the phone. She listened for a moment, then started to yell.

"'No comment' is totally unacceptable!" the editor cried. "I don't care if she is the principal and your mother. I want that story!"

The editor slammed the phone down. Then she faced Ron.

"You're giving me *nothing* here, Stoppable!" she cried. "Where's the edge? The angle? You want to get on the paper?"

Ron and Rufus both nodded.

"Then write a story that makes me care," she told him.

"I'll do it!" Ron exclaimed. "I'm a born reporter. I can smell a story a mile away!"

With great confidence, Ron waited for inspiration to strike.

It was a long wait.

"Maybe Kim has an idea," he finally said.

CHAPTER 2

High School Headlines

Later that day, Ron found Kim on the football field. She was practicing with her cheerleading squad.

"Middleton is H-O-T! Middleton is *hot*. Go, Dogs!" shouted the cheerleaders. The girls jumped and waved their pom-poms.

Kim smiled. As captain, she was glad to see that her squad was ready for this Friday's game. Middleton was playing Eastside, a really tough team. The Mad Dogs were depending on Kim and her squad to cheer them on to *vic-to-ry*!

"Good one, guys," Kim called. When she saw Ron waving at her, she said, "Take five."

"Help me out, K.P.! I need an angle," Ron said, rushing over.

"Why ask me?" asked Kim.

Just then, the football team hurried onto the practice field. Ron ran toward them.

"Okay, okay," Ron called out. "Which one of you guys is failing a class but still playing in this weekend's game?"

The players ignored Ron.

Ron decided he needed a new strategy, so he moved from player to player. "Oh, come on! One of you has to be failing at something," he said eagerly.

This is not good, thought Ron. He could see the Mad Dogs were starting to get *mad*.

On the sidelines, Kim rolled her eyes and turned to pack up her pom-poms. A split second later, a football player tossed Ron across the field. He landed at Kim's feet.

"I've got my story," Ron moaned. "Football team full of nice, great guys who are *not* failing anything."

Suddenly, Brick Flagg, Middleton High's star quarterback, came running up to Kim, stepping right over Ron.

"Hey," he said, tossing his long blond hair.

"Um, hey, Brick," Kim said. She stared at

the big football player, waiting for him to think of something clever to say.

"Uh, nice outfit," he finally told her.

Brilliant, thought Kim. Not! She was wearing the *exact* same cheerleading outfit as every other girl on the squad!

"Uh, thanks," she told Brick with a shrug.

"You know," said Brick, "I think what you do is *really* amazing."

"Ah, saving the world is no big," she said.

Brick shook his head. "I mean how you're always spelling stuff in your cheers. It's so C-O-O-L." Brick giggled, then stopped. He suddenly looked nervous. "That spells cool, right?" he asked.

Kim nodded slowly.

Brick grinned and then trotted back to his team.

Kim sighed and shook her head. Then she saw Ron staring at her. "Why are you looking at me like that?" she asked.

" 'Cause I found my story!" Ron cried. "I'm gonna interview you! *The* Kim Possible."

Kim placed her hands on her hips.

"Since when does my name have a '*the*' in front of it?" she demanded.

But Ron wasn't listening. "Just remember, Kim," he added, "I won't accept anything less than the hard-hitting truth."

CHAPTER 3

Extreme Teen Queen

That night, Kim was sitting on her living room couch with Ron and her twin brothers, Jim and Tim. Ron was supposed to be working on his interview with Kim, but he wanted to watch TV instead. The boys' favorite TV show was on!

Spooky music played over scenes of a dark forest. The night was still. A deserted country road stretched into the distance.

"Tonight," the announcer said in an

13

ominous tone, "one extreme teen will go into the woods alone. No food. No water. No human contact—handcuffed to a bear!"

With an angry roar, a big bear appeared on the television screen. Then came the Extreme Teen Queen herself: Adrena-Lynn. She had short blond hair and a wild look in her pretty, long-lashed eyes.

"That teen is me!" Adrena-Lynn cried. Then she threw up her arms and screamed, *"Freaky!"*

Kim rolled her eyes. "At least the bear won't go hungry," she said.

"And now," said the announcer, "Adrena-Lynn answers the question the whole country is asking!"

"What will she do next!" cried Jim, Tim, and Ron along with the announcer.

Kim sat there in disbelief, then turned to Ron. "I thought you came over to interview me," she said.

"At the *commercial*," Ron replied, his eyes glued to the TV. "Got any chips?"

"Next, Adrena-Lynn and the bear go fishing—for their lives," said the announcer.

Suddenly, the television screen went black.

Kim had grabbed the remote control and turned off the TV.

"KIM!" the boys cried.

Kim's eyes flashed with anger. "This show

is a mind-numbing waste of satellite frequencies," she told them.

"You're right," said Ron. "Besides, I'm taping it at home."

Kim fumed. "Some kid is going to get hurt trying to imitate that girl's stunts," she warned.

"Hey!" Tim cried, suddenly getting an idea. "Let's see if we can sneak into the bear cage at the zoo, like Adrena-Lynn!"

"Cool!" said Jim.

Tim dashed into the kitchen. When he came back, he had a raw steak tied to his head.

"Here, tie this steak on," said Tim. He handed another piece of meat to his brother.

16

"Super cool!" Jim cried.

And they both took off for the zoo. Kim watched the tweebs go with a yawn.

"Aren't you going to stop them?" asked Ron.

"Nah," Kim replied. "The zoo's locked this time of night. All right, let's get this 'hard-hitting' interview over with."

Ron turned on his tape recorder. "So," he began, "what's it like to be you?"

CHAPTER 4

A Freaky Fake

At that very moment, a van rumbled along a dark country road. On the van's roof sat a huge satellite dish. And in the van's passenger seat sat Adrena-Lynn. She was looking through a stack of papers and talking to the van's driver, who also happened to be her cameraman.

"Ratings are up! Merchandise sales are up!" she cried excitedly.

"Copycat incidents are up, too," warned the cameraman.

Adrena-Lynn just laughed. "It means they're watching," she said. "Not my fault if the little dweebs aren't careful."

The cameraman glanced into the rearview mirror at the big bear costume in the back of the van. The "bear" on that night's episode was really just a man in a costume!

"Maybe they don't get it that you fake the stunts," the cameraman said.

"Whatever," Adrena-Lynn replied. "The point is, if we're going to stay on top, the next stunt has to be bigger. More *extreme*!"

The cameraman scratched his head. "Like what?" he asked.

Adrena-Lynn grinned.

"I'm thinking bungee," she said with a wild laugh. *"Freaky!"*

Later that night, Ron sat at the desk in his bedroom. Over and over, he played his tape-recorded interview with Kim. He listened for something exciting, something with an edge, something that would make the school newspaper editor care.

But everything Kim said was so boring!

With a sigh, Ron turned on the tape recorder one more time.

"I'm not so different from anyone else," said Kim's voice. "Except that, you know, I have an arch-foe or two."

Ron looked at Rufus. The mole rat shrugged.

"You're right," Ron said. "After watching Adrena-Lynn wrestle a bear, Kim Possible kind of pales in comparison."

Ron fast-forwarded the tape.

"Sure, I'm busy," said Kim's voice. "But what teenage girl isn't?"

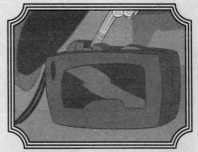

Ron stopped the tape.

"Boring!" he cried, tearing at his hair. "Where's the angle?"

He fast-forwarded the tape a little more.

"It feels good to help people," said Kim.

Rufus made a gagging noise. Ron fast-forwarded the tape again.

"We have an awesome team this year," said Kim. "Brick Flagg was totally hot in last week's game."

Ron blinked. He rewound the tape, then hit PLAY and listened closely.

". . . totally hot," said Kim. "Totally hot . . . totally hot—"

Ron stopped the tape and grinned.

"Houston, the angle has landed!" he cried.

CHAPTER 5

(Heart) Breaking News

The next day, on her way to the cafeteria, Kim got a nasty surprise.

"Kim!" called Bonnie Rockwaller, racing up to her. Bonnie was also on the cheerleading squad, and she was Kim's rival.

Kim tensed when she heard Bonnie's cheerful voice. When Bonnie was happy, somebody somewhere was about to be unhappy. It was Bonnie's Law.

23

"I think it is so great what you did," Bonnie gushed.

"Which was?" Kim asked warily.

"I mean to risk utter embarrassment and  total rejection like that," said Bonnie.

Kim didn't understand, not until Bonnie held up the school newspaper. The headline was huge.

"Cheerleader Kim Possible Thinks Quarterback Brick Flagg is H-O-T, Hot," Kim read aloud. "By Ron Stoppable?"

Kim gasped. She may have said Brick was hot, but only as a football player. Ron's story made it sound like she was crushin' on the guy. But why would Ron lie like that? Kim wondered in horror.

Bonnie patted Kim on the shoulder with fake sympathy. "We'll totally be here for you when he dumps you," she said.

When Kim looked up again, she found herself staring into Brick's face.

"So, Kim, you think I'm hot?" Brick said with a toss of his blond hair.

"Actually," Kim replied, "what I think I said was—"

"Cool," Brick said with a grin. "What are you doing Friday night?"

"Well, nothing," Kim said. "I mean, I mean, nothing with you—"

"Pick you up at eight?" Brick interrupted.

"I . . . uh . . . but—" stuttered Kim.

But Brick was already turning away.

"Hey," he bragged to a friend as he walked down the hallway, "she thinks I'm hot."

Totally embarrassed, Kim ran to the cafeteria where she found Ron in the lunch line. "So I think Brick Flagg is hot?" she cried.

Behind Kim, a girl immediately turned to her friends. "It's true!" she squealed. "Kim just said it herself!"

Kim was way beyond tweaked now. She was totally fuming!

"Did you see it?" asked Ron. He didn't even notice how angry Kim was at him. "My

name in lights. Well, in *ink* actually, but still—"

"Ron!" Kim yelled. "You ferociously misquoted me!"

"Whoa," said Ron. "I may have done a tiny bit of rephrasing, but, come on, you'd think a crime-fighting cheerleader would give a more interesting interview."

Kim glared at Ron.

"The paper liked my story so much they're giving me a *column*," Ron continued. He couldn't see why Kim was so upset. His dream was coming true, and that was *all* he could see.

The cafeteria lady stared at Ron, waiting for his order.

"Uh, I'll have an omelet," Ron said. "Whites only."

The cafeteria lady slapped a plate of gooey muck on his tray.

Ron sighed. In his mind, there was only one reason for this mistake. "She must not know who I am," he said to Kim.

"I'm not sure *I* know who you are," Kim replied.

"So, I'm thinking I should cover the big date with the Brickster," said Ron. "What time should I be ready?"

Before Kim could answer him, Bonnie Rockwaller grabbed Ron's arm.

"Ron!" cried Bonnie. "You're sitting with *us*."

She and another girl started pulling him toward their table.

"I'm having a little get-together tonight," said Bonnie's friend. "No biggie. Just fifty of my closest friends. You have to do a write-up for the paper."

"I do?" said Ron.

"How else will the social outcasts know what they missed?" asked Bonnie.

"You could invite them," suggested Ron.

"You are so funny!" Bonnie giggled. Then she tugged harder on Ron's sleeve.

As Ron walked away with the popular girls, he pointed at Kim and called, "Check you later, K.P." Then he smiled at the girls on each of his arms. "Duty calls."

CHAPTER 6

Stuck on Kim

A few minutes later, Kim sat down at a table by herself. But she wasn't alone for long.

"Hey, Kim. Nice . . . uh . . . lunch," said Brick as he sat down next to her.

"Um, thanks," Kim replied. Then she turned to face Brick. "I'm glad you're here—"

"I'm glad I'm here, too," he interrupted.

But Kim shook her head. "No, no, no, no," she said. "I mean about Friday night. I'm just not sure—"

"If we should go to dinner or a movie?"
Brick said, interrupting her again. "I had the
same debate! But then it hit me—hot dogs at
the theater!"

Kim shook her head again.

Beep, beep! Bee-beep!

It was Kim's Kimmunicator. She took it
out and saw Wade's face on the tiny screen.

Wade was the ten-year-old computer
genius who ran Kim's Web site.

"Save me!" she cried, hoping Wade was
calling about a mission.

Snake-infested jungle? Arctic wasteland?

It didn't matter to Kim *where* Wade was about to send her. *Anything* would be better than going on a date with the dumb-as-a-Brick quarterback!

"Hey," said Brick, leaning over Kim's shoulder to speak to Wade. "You're Kim's computer dude."

"And you're that Kim-thinks-you're-hot dude," replied Wade.

Brick nodded enthusiastically. "Yep, yep, that's me," he crowed.

Kim clenched her teeth, then smiled politely at Brick. She didn't want to hurt his feelings, but she had work to do. "Excuse me, ah, Brick . . . I have to go," Kim said.

As Kim fled the cafeteria, Brick waved. "See ya Friday!" he called loud enough for everyone at Middleton High School to hear.

Kim ran to her locker and threw open the door. Wade's face gazed out at her from the computer screen.

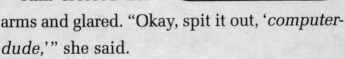

"He seems nice," said Wade.

Kim crossed her arms and glared. "Okay, spit it out, '*computer-dude,*'" she said.

"You got an IM," Wade told Kim. "From Pop-Pop Porter, the frozen food king. He needs your help. Apparently he's been robbed."

Ron suddenly stuck his head around the locker door. "I smell a scoop!" he cried.

Kim elbowed Ron out of the way. "What was stolen?" she demanded.

But Wade had already signed off.

Kim and Ron raced over to Pop-Pop Porter's frozen food factory.

Pop-Pop met them at the entrance to a gigantic hangar. The frozen food king was so upset, he was actually crying.

"My pop-popcorn shrimp!" Pop-Pop sobbed.

Kim frowned. "You brought us out here because someone stole a crustacean?" she

said. "I don't get it." But as Pop-Pop led them farther into the hangar, Kim did.

The hangar was filled with huge floating blimps. Each one was shaped like a different item in Pop-Pop Porter's line of frozen foods. There was a corn dog blimp, a taco blimp, a pig-in-a-blanket blimp, and a sausage blimp.

But in the center of the hangar there was a big empty space. Pop-Pop's famous popcorn shrimp blimp had been stolen!

"Shrimp Force One was my favorite! My favorite!" Pop-Pop cried.

"A blimp should be easy enough to spot," said Ron.

Kim whipped out her Kimmunicator. "Wade, do a search of UFO sightings," she commanded.

"What am I looking for?" Wade asked.

"Anything about Earth being invaded by giant sea creatures," Kim replied.

Wade's fingers danced quickly across his keyboard.

"Let's see," said Wade, gazing at his monitor. "There's a giant pig in Belize. A pterodactyl in Pittsburgh . . ."

Then Wade's eyes went wide. "Wait! I got it!" he cried. "Giant shrimp attacks . . . New York City!"

CHAPTER 7

Blimp Hunt

The streets of New York City were crowded with people enjoying the sights. But Kim and Ron didn't have time for sightseeing. They were on a quest to find a great big gas-filled shrimp!

In the middle of Times Square, Kim glanced down at her Kimmunicator.

"On target, Kim," Wade said. "I'm tracking the blimp just around the corner."

Kim and Ron moved forward. Suddenly,

they heard a familiar voice echoing among the tall buildings.

"*What . . .*" cried the voice from above.

Kim and Ron looked up.

"*What . . .*" boomed the voice again.

"I know that voice," said Kim.

Suddenly the shrimp blimp drifted out from behind a skyscraper. A searchlight played across the floating pink crustacean, highlighting the silhouette of a teenaged girl on the side of the blimp.

"Adrena-Lynn!" Ron cried.

Rufus crawled out of Ron's pocket and on top of Ron's head to get a better look.

Ron and the rest of the crowd that had gathered on the street shouted out Adrena-Lynn's show's slogan, "*What . . .* will she do next?"

"What a story!" Ron cried. "Adrena-Lynn is a real hero."

"Ron! She stole that blimp," Kim reminded him.

Ron shrugged. "This is art," he said. "Sacrifices must be made."

Adrena-Lynn waved to the crowd. She was standing on top of the stolen blimp, her arms outstretched.

"Tonight, I'll attempt the ultimate in extreme action," she announced. "I will bungee jump from this blimp . . ."

"Ooooh," moaned the crowd.

". . . blindfolded! *Freaky!*" cried Adrena-Lynn. Then she jumped.

Down, down, down Adrena-Lynn fell.

Behind her, the bungee cord quickly unwound until it was stretched tight, then—*snap*! The cord broke.

"Whoa!" said Ron, pulling out his camera. Rufus covered his eyes.

Adrena-Lynn plunged toward the pavement.

"Ahhh!" cried Kim. She couldn't believe she would now have to save this silly girl!

With a press of a button, Kim activated her jetpack. The normal-looking backpack transformed itself. Wings appeared, a rocket engine popped out, and a mechanical arm placed a safety helmet on Kim's head.

Then, with a roar, Kim shot into the sky.

Her jetpack blazing, she raced to catch
Adrena-Lynn before she hit the sidewalk.

"Gotcha!" cried Kim as she swooped in to
catch the falling girl.

But as Kim swerved to avoid hitting a
building, she looked down at the limp form
in her arms. A gust of wind blew the blond
wig and blindfold away—and Kim saw that
she wasn't holding Adrena-Lynn. She was
holding a sack of sand in sporty clothing.

Kim had risked her life for a *dummy*!

"Okay, that's really annoying," said Kim,
landing on a nearby roof.

Then a voice boomed over the crowd. *"Freaky!"*

"She's okay!" roared the announcer.

"She made it!" cried Ron.

Just then, searchlights pointed up to the roof of a tall building. Standing there, unharmed, Adrena-Lynn threw up her arms and did a victory dance.

Ron Stoppable pointed his camera at the teen idol. He zoomed in for a close-up and snapped a picture of Adrena-Lynn.

"Rufus, my friend," said Ron. "Guess who got a front-page photo?"

"You?" asked Rufus.

Ron moved his camera around until he found Kim. She was standing on the very next roof—and she was holding something. Ron focused in and then gasped.

Kim was holding an Adrena-Lynn dummy!

"Oh, no!" Ron cried. "It can't be . . . it was just a dummy. She didn't even fall."

Ron snapped photo after photo. He couldn't believe it. His hero, Extreme Teen Queen Adrena-Lynn, was a fake!

CHAPTER 8

Ron Stoppable, Ace Reporter

The next day, Ron returned to Middleton High School sad and depressed. He leaned against the wall of lockers, eyes downcast.

When Kim saw him, she shook her head and told him, "Ron, get over it already."

"Sorry, K.P.," Ron moaned. "But discovering that your action hero is a big fake is not something you just 'get over.'"

Kim sighed. "And this from a *wrestling* fan?"

Ron frowned. "I don't get the connection," he said.

Kim rolled her eyes and yanked open her locker  door. Wade's face immediately appeared on her computer screen.

"Looks like Pop-Pop Porter got so much publicity he's not pressing charges for the blimp theft," Wade said with a grin.

Ron was shocked. "So she's getting away with it?" he said.

"Well, I *was* able to highlight the key areas on that photo-file," Wade told him.

With a mechanical hum, the printer spit out a page. Ron grabbed it and scanned the photos he'd taken the night before. One showed Adrena-Lynn dancing on the rooftop. Kim could be seen in the background, holding the fake Adrena-Lynn.

Ron shook his head. "She called herself '*Extreme*'?" he said. "The big fake."

"Imagine that!" said Kim. "Lying to the public just to build up your *own* reputation."

Maybe now Ron would *finally* see what he'd done with that stupid Brick story, thought Kim. But Ron remained as clueless as ever.

"Disgusting!" was all he said in reply. Then he stomped his foot.

"Well, Adrena-Lynn might get a pass from Pop-Pop," he declared, "but Ron Stoppable smells a story!"

The news that Adrena-Lynn, the Extreme Teen Queen, was a phony made the front page of the Middleton High newspaper that very afternoon. By the end  of the day, the shocking truth made national headlines, as well.

To Ron Stoppable's delight, his name appeared in newspapers all across the nation. Overnight, he went from a back-page zero to a news-hound hero!

And the fame went straight to his head. By the next day, Ron was totally full of himself.

When Kim opened her locker that morning, a TV announcer appeared on her computer screen, talking about—who else? Ron Stoppable!

"Ron Stoppable of the Middleton High

newspaper reports that Extreme Teen Adrena-Lynn is an extreme *fake*," said the announcer.

Then Ron appeared at Kim's locker. He showed Kim the front page of *The Examiner*.

"I'm in the paper," he crowed. "I'm national, baby!"

Kim could not believe her eyes. She read the headline out loud just to make sure it was real. "Ace reporter Ron Stoppable heralded for breaking the story of TV fake. Adrena-

Lynn's ratings plummet faster than her fake fall."

Kim looked up from the paper. Ron was grinning—totally pleased with himself. *He* had become the *star* of his own news story.

"Can this get any more annoying?" Kim asked.

Just then, her Kimmunicator chirped. Wade appeared on the screen.

"What's up, Wade?" asked Kim.

Wade looked tense, his expression grim. Kim knew something very bad had happened even before Wade spoke.

"It's . . . it's your brothers," Wade said ominously.

CHAPTER 9

Copycat Calamity

Kim found her brothers at the Middleton Hospital Emergency Room. They were sitting on a hospital bed. Tim's leg was in a cast and Jim wore a sling around his arm.

Kim's mother and father were at the hospital, too. Like Kim, they were very upset.

"You were doing *what*?" Kim cried.

"Bungee jumping out of a blimp, like Adrena-Lynn," said Jim as he high-fived Tim.

50

"Only we didn't have a blimp, so we used the roof," Tim explained.

"And we didn't have a bungee cord, so we used yarn," Jim added.

Kim's father was furious. "That Adrena-Lynn is a menace!" he cried.

Kim's mother shook her head. "And she didn't really bungee jump out of a blimp. Don't you boys watch the news?" she asked.

"Nah," said Jim. "The only show we watch is Adrena-Lynn."

Then Jim glanced at the clock. "Hey, it's time!" he cried, clicking the TV remote.

Though the TV came on, Adrena-Lynn did

not. Instead, a television announcer was speaking to the audience.

". . . and reports that Adrena-Lynn is a fake," said the announcer, "coupled with a rash of copycat stunts across the country—"

"Hey, that's us!" Tim cried proudly.

Jim and Tim high-fived again.

"Ow!" Jim cried. His arm was sore!

The announcer continued. "—has prompted this network to cancel Adrena-Lynn in favor of more responsible programming. So stay tuned to an extra hour of *Stuff on Fire.*"

Jim and Tim stared at the TV, totally stunned.

Kim turned off the television. "Excellent," she said. "Now I can focus on the looming disaster in my social life."

After school that day, the cheerleaders began practicing a new cheer for Friday's big game.

"Hip to the left!" they yelled. "Hip to the right, spin and slide." The cheerleaders waved their pom-poms.

"Who's gonna win against Eastside? Who? Who?" Kim continued, finishing the cheer.

Suddenly, Ron, wearing black shades, strode down the side of the football field. He was followed by a crowd of people.

Ron gave Kim a thumb's-up sign. "Lookin' good, K.P.," he said.

Kim took in Ron's sunglasses and the fans surrounding him. She frowned.

"Oh, don't worry, baby," said Ron. "I'm not going to forget the *little* people who got me where I am today. I'll be there Friday night to cover your date with Brick. Oh, yeah!"

"Cool," said Brick Flagg, walking past. "Our date's gonna be, like . . . newsworthy."

Brick kept walking. Kim tried to stop him. "Brick, wait! We need to talk," she said.

Brick spun around. His face suddenly fell and he looked pale.

"Did you just say 'we need to talk'?" Brick asked nervously.

Kim nodded yes.

Brick's lower lip began to quiver. "That's exactly what Amelia said last year when

she dumped me—I mean, when we, you know, broke up," Brick said in a shaky voice.

Kim gulped. "Well," she said, "you can't really call it *breaking up* if we haven't even—"

Brick's shoulders slumped. "I was a wreck," he confessed. "I totally blew it in the big game against Eastside."

Then Brick looked at Kim. "So, what did you want to talk to me about?"

Kim stared at Brick. "Just that . . . I can't wait for Friday either," she found herself saying to him.

This is *so* not good, thought Kim, but the game against Eastside *is* the most important one of the year. The entire student body would hate her if they found out *she* was the reason their star quarterback couldn't play.

"Cool," said Brick with a toss of his blond hair.

When Brick wandered back to his team-mates, Kim shook her head.

"I am *so* toast!" she cried.

CHAPTER 10

Extreme Teen's Revenge

"She is *so* toast!" Adrena-Lynn cried.

The Extreme Teen Queen was behind the wheel of her van. As she drove down the highway, she turned to the cameraman sitting next to her and said, "Roll the camera."

"*Hello*, Adrena-Lynn," replied the cameraman, "we've been canceled."

Adrena-Lynn went crazy. "We're not canceled until *I* say we're canceled!" she shouted, pounding the steering wheel.

The cameraman shrugged and pointed the camera at Adrena-Lynn.

"A lonely highway. A desperate mission," said Adrena-Lynn, staring into the camera lens. "Tonight I will pull my greatest stunt yet—revenge against Kim Possible and Ron Stoppable!"

The cameraman stopped filming, and Adrena-Lynn grinned.

"How's that for a teaser?" she asked.

"Good," he replied. "It'd be *better* if we had an audience."

Adrena-Lynn's eyes narrowed. "Oh, we will," she promised.

* * *

At the same time, Kim was walking through the halls of Middleton High School. When she suddenly heard the pay phone ring, she picked it up.

"Hello?" said Kim.

"Kim!" cried a familiar voice. "This is Wade. Sorry to use a landline, but the Kimmunicator satellite is down."

"What's the sitch?" Kim asked.

"It's not *just* the Kimmunicator," Wade replied. "Video signals all over the world are getting messed up."

There was a crisis afoot, and no peace and quiet for Kim at home, either. The Possible house was in an uproar. A terrible tragedy had occurred.

"Darn TV!" exclaimed Kim's father as he tried to get a picture.

"Whack it again, Dad!" Jim cried.

"You *have* to make it work," moaned Tim. "What good is having a broken leg if you can't sit and watch TV all day?"

"Maybe this is a good thing," said Kim's mother. "We can have some quality family time."

Jim and Tim considered her words for a minute. Then they turned to their father.

"Dad, *please!*" Jim cried.

"You're a rocket scientist!" cried Tim, just as desperately. "Can't you *do* something?"

"Well, I could put it in geosynchronous orbit, but I'm not sure how that would help," Mr. Possible replied.

Then Kim arrived.

"Oh, Kimmie, your boyfriend called while you were out," said her mother.

"He's not my boyfriend!" Kim insisted.

"That's not what Ron said in *The Ron Report*," said Kim's mother.

Kim moaned and sank into a chair. Her mother sat down next to her and asked, "Is something wrong, honey?"

"You have our undivided attention," said her father.

Kim looked up, amazed.

"The TV's broken," her father explained.

Kim sighed. "Ron made up a story about

me liking the quarterback, and now I'm stuck dating him or we'll lose the big game. Meanwhile, there's a worldwide satellite crisis." Kim put her head in her hands.

For a moment, Kim's mom thought over her daughter's problems. "Kimmie, you have to be honest with Brick," she advised. "If the football team loses, it's not your fault." After a pause, she added, "I can't help you with the satellite thing."

Just then, Jim pointed to the television, which was suddenly working again.

"Ah, I don't think you have to worry about dating Brick tonight," said Jim.

On the screen they saw a close-up of Brick. There was a look of confusion on his face. Then the camera pulled

back to reveal Adrena-Lynn standing next to him.

"Hey," said Brick. "I thought you said Kim wanted to meet me here?"

Adrena-Lynn looked directly into the camera. "Oh, she'll be here," the Extreme Teen Queen said with an evil grin.

"Adrena-Lynn!" Tim and Jim cried.

"Hmmm," said Kim's father. "I thought she was canceled."

He hit a button on the remote and the channel changed. Adrena-Lynn and Brick were on the next channel, too. And the next. In fact, they were on *every* channel!

"Well," said Kim, "I think we know

who's jamming the satellite transmissions."

Kim pulled out her Kimmunicator.

"Wade?" she said.

But Wade wasn't there. Adrena-Lynn and Brick were even on the Kimmunicator's screen!

"Tonight: Ron Stoppable and Kim Possible versus me—in extreme combat!" Adrena-Lynn cried. "And to raise the stakes, I have Kim's boyfriend."

"He is *not* my boyfriend!" Kim declared.

Her entire family was staring at her.

Kim sighed, got up, and grabbed her back-pack. "Don't worry, I'm going," she said.

CHAPTER 11

Crisis at the Carnival

A few minutes later, Kim and Ron were on Ron's scooter driving down a dark road.

"Kim, the only thing down this road is the old Middleton Fairgrounds," Ron said.

"That and Adrena-Lynn," Kim replied.

"That place is haunted," Ron whined. "Plus I lost, like, ten bucks trying to win a stuffed hippo."

"Too bad, Ron," said Kim. "If it weren't for you and your stories, we wouldn't be here."

Ron and Kim arrived at the fairgrounds. All around them the carnival rides were dark. Leaves blew in the night wind.

"This place gives me the creeps," whispered Ron as he and Kim walked down the midway. A wolf howled in the woods and Ron yelped.

"Creepy!" squeaked Rufus as he dived into Ron's pocket.

Suddenly, the lights on the midway went on. Carnival music filled the night. The merry-go-round began to spin. And in the distance, an old roller coaster lit up.

Brick sat in a car at the top of the roller coaster, tied up.

"High school quarterback Brick Flagg takes the ride of his life!" cried the Extreme Teen Queen. Adrena-Lynn stood at the roller

coaster's controls, ready to throw the lever. A spotlight illuminated a hole in the tracks near the end of the ride. If Adrena-Lynn pulled that switch, it would be the *last* ride Brick ever took!

"And the only person who can save him," continued Adrena-Lynn, "is his beloved girl-friend, Kim Possible!"

"And me," squeaked Ron, cowering behind Kim.

"Drop the dramatics, Adrena-Lynn!" called Kim. "This isn't a game."

"Exactly," said Adrena-Lynn. "It's real. It's extreme. And it's *freaky*!"

At that moment, Adrena-Lynn pulled the lever, and Brick's car began to roll down the track.

"Clock's ticking," said Adrena-Lynn.

"Come on, Ron!" cried Kim.

But before they could move, Adrena-Lynn activated a conveyor belt beneath them. In the wink of an eye, Kim and Ron were dragged helplessly into the Fun House. Flipping end over end, they plunged into a tunnel, and were then unceremoniously dumped into the Room of Fun House Mirrors.

Each and every mirror reflected Adrena-Lynn's image.

"Gee, I wonder how the quarterback is doing?" shouted Adrena-Lynn. Then she started laughing.

Kim kicked at the Adrena-Lynn closest to her—but her foot merely bounced off the glass.

We've got to get out of here, thought Kim. But when she and Ron tried to run, the floor wobbled under their feet. Then they fell through a trapdoor and into another tunnel.

"Whoa!" screamed Ron.

"Whoa!" cried Kim.

This time when they landed, they found

themselves in the middle of a bumper car arena.

"Look out, Ron!" Kim cried. Adrena-Lynn was driving a bumper car right at them. Just in time, Kim shoved Ron out of the way.

Then Adrena-Lynn's cameraman rolled

past them. He was riding in his own bumper car and filming everything so the whole world could see.

Behind the cameraman, Kim could see Brick hurtling down the roller coaster tracks. Time was running out!

"Kim?" said Adrena-Lynn in a phony-surprised voice. "Playing *games* when poor

Brick is hurtling toward his doom? What kind of girlfriend are you?"

Kim jumped out of the way as Adrena-Lynn tried to run her over again.

Across town, the Possible family was watching Kim's every move on TV.

"That girl doesn't play fair!" cried Kim's dad.

"Come on, Kimmie!" shouted Kim's mother. "Show 'em what you've got!"

"Go get her, Adrena-Lynn!" countered Jim.

"Jim! Tim!" scolded their father. "There'll be no rooting for your sister's foe."

CHAPTER 12

Reality Check

Back at the fairgrounds, Kim jumped into a bumper car. After a couple of tries, she was finally able to knock Adrena-Lynn out of her car and out of the bumper car arena. Then she ran over to the roller coaster to save Brick. As Kim climbed the roller coaster's frame, she heard the frightened voice of Ron—

"Kim!" he shouted.

Kim turned and discovered that Ron had been tied to a seat on the Spinning Swings

ride. Adrena-Lynn pressed a button and the ride began to turn.

"Ahh!" howled Ron.

Faster and faster the swings spun. The ride was old, and some of the ropes began to snap.

"No, please," begged Ron. "This ride always makes me throw up!"

Kim glanced up at Brick. He still had a little time before his roller coaster car hit the hole in the tracks. She had to save Ron first.

Kim grabbed some long, colorful streamers and swung off the roller coaster. When she hit the ground, she turned off the swing ride. But as she started to untie Ron, Adrena-Lynn laughed evilly.

"That move's gonna cost you," she said, surprising Kim by swinging down from one of the broken ropes and pushing her into a passing cable car.

Up Kim went on the cable car, higher and higher.

"The quarterback's almost out of time, and you're going the wrong way!" Adrena-Lynn taunted.

"Adrena-Lynn, you cannot do this!" Ron cried, still tied to the swing ride.

"And why not?" she asked.

"I'm the one responsible for your show being canceled. I called you a fake," said Ron. "Well, I guess it takes one to know one.

I made up that stuff about Kim liking Brick just to sell my story."

"Oh, harsh," said Brick, overhearing Ron's confession.

"It worked, kind of," said Ron. "But the thing is, if the fake part about you is what people like . . . well, what good is that?"

Adrena-Lynn thought for a moment. "You're right," she said.

"From now on, I'm keeping it real," Ron promised.

"Me, too," said Adrena-Lynn. "Starting with my very *real* defeat of Kim Possible!"

As Adrena-Lynn laughed maniacally, Ron shrugged. "Okay, *that* didn't work," he said.

Meanwhile, time was really running out for Brick. Kim activated her jetpack and blasted right out of the cable car ride.

Brick's roller coaster car was racing down the final stretch. Just as his car plunged through the hole in the tracks, Kim scooped Brick up.

The car smashed to the ground and exploded. But Brick was safe and sound in Kim's arms. She set him down next to Adrena-Lynn and Ron.

"Let's see," said Kim. "What will *I* do next?"

Then Kim scooped up Adrena-Lynn and, using her jetpack, blasted off. In seconds, they were both flying high over the fairgrounds.

"I do extreme stunts for a living," snapped Adrena-Lynn. "You think I'm afraid of heights?"

"You do *fake* extreme stunts," corrected Kim. "Let the world see how brave you are when there's *real* danger."

With her jetpack blasting, Kim flew even higher into the air. Then she did a double loop. Over and over again.

Wide-eyed, Adrena-Lynn went pale.

"Not so extreme after all now, are you?" Kim asked. But Adrena-Lynn was too frightened to reply.

"*Are you?*" Kim demanded.

"No!" Adrena-Lynn finally admitted in front of her worldwide audience.

Watching from their living room, Tim and Jim gasped in shock.

"*Now* she tells us," they said, frowning at their bandaged limbs.

When Kim landed again, the police were waiting. And Adrena-Lynn and her cameraman were hauled away in handcuffs.

Finally, Kim turned to Brick. "Listen," she said, "I'm sorry you almost plunged to your death on worldwide television—"

"Kim, stop. I get it now," he interrupted.

"You do?" asked Kim.

"Sure. You had that skinny guy expose Adrena-Lynn so she'd freak out and set up this whole 'save Brick' thing, just to prove you dug me," Brick said.

Kim could not believe her ears.

"Kim, you're nice and all," he continued, "but you try too hard. If you'd just asked me out, that's cool. But this is too much."

Brick touched Kim's shoulder. "I'm sorry," he said. "But it's over."

Then Brick walked away. Kim watched him go, her mouth open in disbelief.

After all she'd done for the guy, *he* had the nerve to dump *her*!

"I can't believe it!" Ron cried.

"I know!" Kim said.

But Ron wasn't listening. He was thinking about what a story *this* news was going to make. "Headline!" he shouted. *"Quarterback sacks Kim Possible. She has a dislocated heart and will be out for the remainder of the season—"*

Before he could say another word, Rufus covered Ron's mouth with his paws.

"Thank you," said Kim, relieved that someone had finally shut Ron up!